QUEEN SUE LOVED BLUE

By Kristine Humer
Illustrated by Matt Phillips

BARRON'S

Table of Contents

Illustration on page 21 by InContext Publishing Partners;
Illustrations on pages 22–23 by Deborah Gross

All inquiries should be addressed to:
Barron's Educational Series, Inc.
250 Wireless Boulevard
Hauppauge, New York 11788
www.barronseduc.com

Library of Congress Catalog Card No.: 2006028824
ISBN-13: 978-0-7641-3724-2
ISBN-10: 0-7641-3724-7

Library of Congress Cataloging-in-Publication Data
Humer, Kristine.
    Queen Sue loved blue / by Kristine Humer.
    p. cm. — (Reader's clubhouse)

    ISBN-13: 978-0-7641-3724-2
    ISBN-10: 0-7641-3724-7
    1. Reading—Phonetic method. 2. Readers (Primary)   I. Title.

LB1573.3.H86 2007
372.46'5—dc22

                                                            2006028824

PRINTED IN CHINA
9 8 7 6 5 4 3 2 1

Dear Parent and Educator,

Welcome to the Barron's Reader's Clubhouse, a series of books that provide a phonics approach to reading.

Phonics is the relationship between letters and sounds. It is a system that teaches children that letters have specific sounds. Level 1 books introduce the short-vowel sounds. Level 2 books progress to the long-vowel sounds. Level 3 books then go on to vowel combinations and words ending in "y." This progression matches how phonics is taught in many classrooms.

Queen Sue Loved Blue introduces the "ue" and "ew" vowel combination sound. Simple words with these vowel combinations are called **decodable words.** The child knows how to sound out these words because he or she has learned the sound they include. This story also contains **high-frequency words.** These are common, everyday words that the child learns to read by sight. High-frequency words help ensure fluency and comprehension. **Challenging words** go a little beyond the reading level. The child may need help from an adult to understand these words. All words are listed by their category on page 24.

Here are some coaching and prompting statements you can use to help a young reader read *Queen Sue Loved Blue:*

- **On page 5, "Drew" is a decodable word. Point to the word and say:**

  Read this word. How did you know the word? What sounds did it make?

  Note: There are many opportunities to repeat the above instruction throughout the book.

- **On page 4, "statue" is a challenging word. Point to the word and say:**

  Read this word. Sound out the word. How did you know the word? What helped you?

You'll find more coaching ideas on the Reader's Clubhouse Web site: *www.barronsclubhouse.com.* Reader's Clubhouse is designed to teach and reinforce reading skills in a fun way. We hope you enjoy helping children discover their love of reading!

Sincerely,

Nancy Harris

Nancy Harris
Reading Consultant

Queen Sue loved all things
blue. Every house and statue
around had to be blue.

Queen Sue loved bluebirds.
She loved blue food. Most of
all, Queen Sue loved her dog,
Drew. And yes, Drew was
blue, too.

One day, Queen Sue saw a jewel. It was so blue! Queen Sue got the blue jewel. Then she asked, What shall I do with the blue jewel?

Drew knew. Your crown needs
the blue jewel, said Drew. He
used a lot of glue.

Oh no! said Queen Sue. Now my crown will not come off! Drew, what shall we do?

Drew knew. I will chew, said
Drew. The crown would not
move. What shall we do?
asked Queen Sue.

Drew knew. Drew found a crew
to help.

There was too much glue.
Queen Sue asked, What shall
we do?

Drew knew. Drew said, I will
go find Prue.

Prue lived where there was blue. There were other hues, too.

Prue said, I have a clue.
Prue made a stew. It might
work on glue.

Queen Sue looked at the stew.
Could this stew work on glue?
She asked Drew, What shall
I do?

I wish I knew, said Drew. This
stew looks good. It might take
away the glue. The stew might
rescue you.

Down came the cold stew on the head of Queen Sue. I hope it will work, said Sue. I hope your stew will take away this glue.

Sue's wish came true! The
crown came off. Then the jewel
came off. Thank you, thank
you, said happy Queen Sue.

Queen Sue and Drew love
blue. Now, they also love red,
and green, and other hues,
too.

Fun Facts About

Blue

- The sapphire is a blue jewel. It is the birthstone for people born in September.

- The state of Maine is the largest producer of blueberries in the world.

- The bluebird is a beautiful bird. It helps humans. Bluebirds eat insects that damage crops and gardens.

- People use *blue* in phrases that mean both good and bad things. If you win a contest you might receive a *blue ribbon*. But if you are feeling sad, you might say you're *feeling blue*.

• Blue is one of the three primary colors. The others are red and yellow. All other colors are made from a mix of the primary colors.

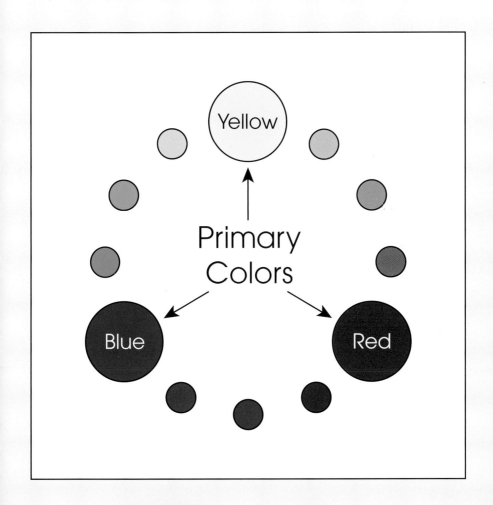

Mixing Primary Colors

Many colors are a mixture of different amounts of red, yellow, and blue. This activity will help you see how colors are formed by mixing the primary colors.

You will need:

- paper (thick, white paper made for painting)
- red, blue, and yellow paint (finger paints will work best, but water paints will work too)
- smock to protect your clothing

1. Paint a large red circle mostly on the left side of the paper.

2. Before the red paint dries, paint a blue circle on the right side. Make the two circles overlap. What color do you see where the red and blue circles mix?

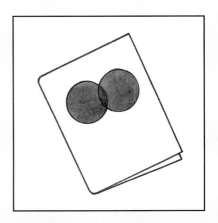

3. Paint a yellow circle overlapping the red and blue circles. What new colors do you see?

4. Try this several more times. Mix different amounts of the colors. What happens when you use a tiny bit of one color and a lot of another?

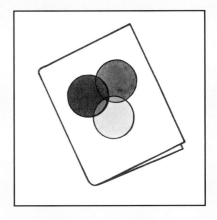

Word List

Challenging Words

crew	jewel	rescue
crown	queen	statue

Decodable ue & ew Words

blue	glue	Sue
bluebirds	hues	Sue's
chew	knew	true
clue	Prue	
Drew	stew	

High-Frequency Words

a	good	most	the
all	got	move	then
also	green	my	there
and	had	much	they
around	happy	needs	things
asked	have	no	this
at	he	not	to
away	head	now	too
be	help	of	used
came	her	off	was
cold	hope	oh	we
come	house	on	were
could	I	one	what
day	it	other	where
do	lived	red	will
dog	looked	said	wish
down	looks	saw	with
every	lot	shall	work
find	love	she	would
food	loved	so	yes
found	made	take	you
go	might	thank	your